Stories to Grow By

The Suspicious Stranger

A Tale in Which Kindness Is Repaid

by Kathryn Wheeler
Illustrated by Julie Anderson

In Celebration™, Grand Rapids, MI

Library of Congress Cataloging-in-Publication Data

Wheeler, Kathryn, 1954-
    The suspicious stranger : a tale in which kindness is repaid / by Kathryn Wheeler ;
illustrated by Julie Anderson.
        p. cm. -- (Stories to grow by)
    Summary: All the squirrels except Sally shun the strange new neighbor, but Sally's
kindness is repaid when Squeak saves her life. Includes a Bible verse and facts about squirrels.
    ISBN 1-56822-592-X (hard cover)
        [1. Squirrels--Fiction. 2. Kindness--Fiction. 3. Christian life--Fiction.] I. Anderson,
Julie, ill. II. Title. III. Series.

PZ7.W5655 Su 2000
[E]--dc21
                                                                                    00-022232

Credits

Author: Kathryn Wheeler
Cover and Inside Illustrations: Julie Anderson
Project Director/Editor: Alyson Kieda

ISBN: 1-56822-592-X
The Suspicious Stranger
Copyright © 1999 by In Celebration®
a division of Instructional Fair Group, Inc.
a Tribune Education Company
3195 Wilson Drive NW
Grand Rapids, Michigan 49544

For information regarding permission write to:
In Celebration®, P.O. Box 1650, Grand Rapids, MI 49501.

Printed in Singapore

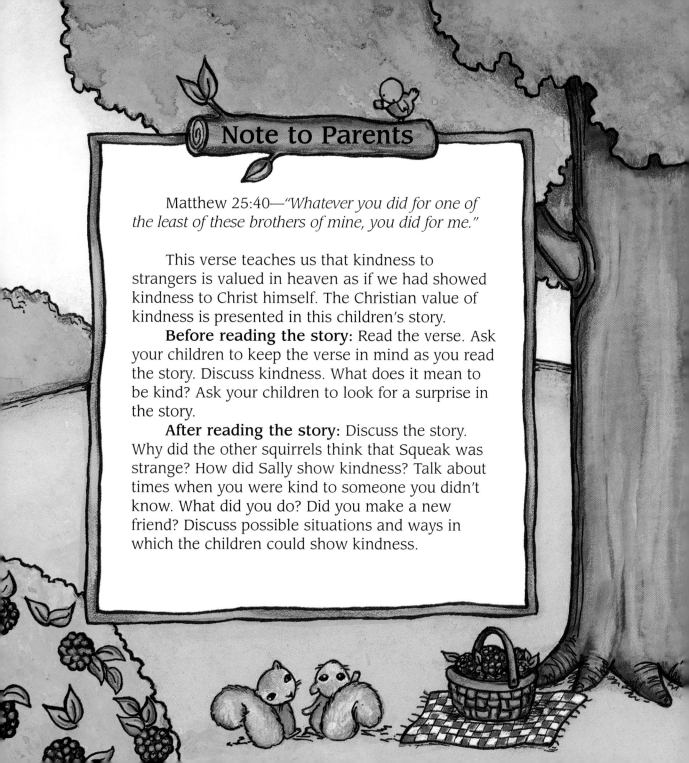

Note to Parents

Matthew 25:40—*"Whatever you did for one of the least of these brothers of mine, you did for me."*

This verse teaches us that kindness to strangers is valued in heaven as if we had showed kindness to Christ himself. The Christian value of kindness is presented in this children's story.

Before reading the story: Read the verse. Ask your children to keep the verse in mind as you read the story. Discuss kindness. What does it mean to be kind? Ask your children to look for a surprise in the story.

After reading the story: Discuss the story. Why did the other squirrels think that Squeak was strange? How did Sally show kindness? Talk about times when you were kind to someone you didn't know. What did you do? Did you make a new friend? Discuss possible situations and ways in which the children could show kindness.

"Psst! Did you hear about that new squirrel, Sally?" called out Freddy Squirrel from his tree. "He's very strange."

"Strange?" Sally stopped sweeping her front doorstep to listen.

Freddy shrugged. "He's . . . well . . . he's not like us."

Sally's Aunt Bertha called out from her tree, "He has huge, dark, beady eyes."

Sam Squirrel, who was down on the grass burying a nut, nodded and called out, "He's small and sneaky. I haven't seen him once since he moved into the hickory tree."

Sally sighed and put her broom away. Her neighbors were always so nervous about newcomers. "I'll try to make this squirrel welcome," she decided. "I'll take him some rose-leaf tea."

After Sally polished her walnut collection and made her bed, she put some tea in an acorn canister and took it over to the hickory tree. She knocked at the knothole door. "Anyone home?" she called.

6

There was a rustling and a bustling, and then the door burst open. Sally blinked in surprise. The little squirrel, dressed in very flashy pajamas, had obviously been asleep! In the middle of the day!

Sally stammered, "I . . . I'm your new neighbor, Sally. I brought you some tea."

The small gray squirrel just stared. Finally he took the acorn canister. "Uhh, thanks," he murmured drowsily as he closed the door.

Sally was appalled. Asleep during the day! Why wasn't he busy burying nuts and looking for berries? And now that she thought about it, the little squirrel wasn't at all polite. He practically shut the door in her face!

That evening, just
after Sally had pulled up her feather
quilt and settled into her pine-straw bed,
there was a knock on the door. It was the
strange little squirrel. "Oh, I'm sorry if I woke you," he said.
"I wanted to thank you again for the tea. I was very sleepy before.
And I didn't introduce myself. My name is Squeak."

Sally grabbed the little squirrel and
pulled him indoors. "What are you doing
out at night?" she cried. "Don't you know
how dangerous it is?"

Squeak blurted, "But I always look for food
at night!"

"There are owls and other scary animals out
there," said Sally.

"An owl would have a hard time catching
me," Squeak replied.

After Squeak had left, Sally went back to bed, puzzled about the strange squirrel. She wasn't quite sure what to make of him. "Could he be an orphan?" she wondered. "Maybe he didn't have a mother to teach him properly." Then Sally had a brilliant idea. "I know! I'll leave him a note and ask if he'd like to food-hunt with me. I could give him some lessons."

In the morning, Sally slipped her note under Squeak's knothole door, not wanting to wake him again. Then she went out to take an inventory of her buried food. "One acorn . . . check. One crab apple . . . check," she said under her breath, sniffing the ground. She was so busy she didn't hear Aunt Bertha pad up behind her.

10

"Sally!" Sally jumped and turned. Her aunt waddled closer and whispered, "I found out more about that odd little squirrel. Did you know that he leaves his nest after sunset and . . . and sleeps all day? Did you ever hear of such a thing? There's something very strange about that one. I say we steer clear of him!"

Sally sighed. "I think he just needs help." Before Bertha could argue, Sally handed her a crab apple. Bertha waddled away munching happily.

The next morning, Sally
found a birch bark note under her door. "No need
to worry about me," Squeak had written. "I'm
fine. Perhaps I could take you out some night to
hunt with me by the light of the moon."

Sally sighed again. "Well, I've done
my best to help," she thought, and
went out to look for food.

12

That day, Sally had good luck. She stumbled onto a new patch of blackberries. She spent all day hiding the berries, one by one. Sally worked so hard she didn't notice the sun going down. And she definitely didn't hear the sound of shifting feet in the bushes behind her. "Blackberries all winter," she hummed happily. When Sally had picked the last gleaming berry, she sat down to eat it for her supper.

Suddenly, the air was filled with a strange whoosh. Sally gasped. It was Squeak! He had jumped off a high branch. But instead of falling, he sailed through the air. Squeak could fly!

"Didn't you hear me calling? There's a fox! Hurry!" Squeak said as he yanked Sally onto the trunk of a tree. They scrambled up the bark just as a fox jumped out from the bushes, jaws snapping.

14

Sally struggled onto a high branch and gasped, "Thank you, Squeak. You . . . you saved my life. How did you do it? Why didn't you fall when you jumped? You are a squirrel, aren't you?"

Squeak laughed. "I sure am. I'm a flying squirrel." He stretched out one of his front and back legs and showed her the flap of skin between them. "This works like a wing," he said.

15

"Wow!
Is that why you
aren't afraid of owls?"
    Squeak nodded.
"But I am afraid of foxes!" he said,
looking at the red triangle of a face far
below them.
    "How can I ever repay you?"
asked Sally.
    "No need," said Squeak.
"I'm repaying you for your
kindness. You are the only one
who has made friends with me."

16

"The others will too," Sally promised. "I'll tell them how you saved me." She handed Squeak half of the berry she still had with her. "Care for some supper?"

Squeak smiled in thanks. "I don't get many blackberries," he said. "They're hard to see in the dark."

17

After they ate, the new friends
chattered at the fox and threw leaves down
at his face until he gave up and slunk away.
Sally raced home as the stars came out and
the moon rose. As Sally scurried, Squeak
flew from branch to branch, guiding his
friend safely to her front door.

18

A Note About Squirrels

Squirrels are native to every continent except Australia and Antarctica. They are known for their energy and curiosity.

There are several breeds of squirrels in North America, but one of the most prevalent is the fox squirrel. These tree-climbing squirrels can weigh up to 6½ pounds (3 kilograms). They have orange coloration and pointed, foxlike ears. They are active during the day, hunting for nuts, seeds, berries, and buds in the early morning and late afternoon. Like all squirrels, fox squirrels set aside part of their food to prepare for the winter. In the late summer and early fall, they take inventory every day to ensure that their food caches are large enough to help them survive the winter. They are tidy animals who spend considerable time grooming themselves and cleaning their nests. Fox squirrels are careful to return to their nests each evening before sunset in order to avoid predators.

Flying squirrels are also tree-climbing squirrels, with folds of skin between their front and back legs. These "wings" allow them to glide long distances, and they use their tails as rudders when they glide from tree to tree. Flying squirrels are soft brown in color, with white underbellies and large brown eyes. They are small squirrels, weighing from ¾ ounces to 5½ pounds (22 grams to 2.5 kilograms).

Flying squirrels cannot fly like birds; they can only glide from a higher point to a lower one, and must climb trees like other squirrels to seek refuge in high branches. As nocturnal animals, flying squirrels sleep during the day and go out every night after sunset to look for food. They have double the defenses of regular squirrels—they can run swiftly and also fly away from predators such as owls. Although flying squirrels live in many parts of North America, we seldom see them, since they are extremely shy and cautious around humans.